Teach Your Buffalo to Play Drums

Gianna—

March to your own beat!

Audrey Vernick

Written by **Audrey Vernick** • Illustrated by **Daniel Jennewein**

Balzer + Bray
An Imprint of HarperCollins *Publishers*

Balzer + Bray is an imprint of HarperCollins Publishers.

Teach Your Buffalo to Play Drums

Text copyright © 2011 by Audrey Vernick

Illustrations copyright © 2011 by Daniel Jennewein

Manufactured in China. All rights reserved.

No part of this book may be used or reproduced in any manner whatsoever without

written permission except in the case of brief quotations embodied in critical

articles and reviews. For information address HarperCollins Children's Books, a

division of HarperCollins Publishers, 10 East 53rd Street, New York, NY 10022.

www.harpercollinschildrens.com

Library of Congress Cataloging-in-Publication Data

Vernick, Audrey.

    Teach your buffalo to play drums / written by Audrey Vernick ; illustrated by Daniel

Jennewein. — 1st ed.

        p.   cm.

    Summary: Encourages the reader, through practical and humorous advice, to

support his or her buffalo's desire to play the drums, even if he has quickly lost interest

in other activities in the past.

        ISBN 978-0-06-176253-6 (trade bdg.) — ISBN 978-0-06-176255-0 (lib. bdg.)

        [1. Drum—Fiction.   2. Musicians—Fiction.   3. Buffaloes—Fiction.

4. Humorous stories.]   I. Jennewein, Daniel, ill.   II. Title.

PZ7.V5973Te   2010   2010007478

[E]—dc22   CIP

                                                                        AC

Typography by Martha Rago

11 12 13 14 15 SCP 10 9 8 7 6 5 4 3 2 1

First Edition

In memory of my mother,
Judy Glassman, who taught me
everything

—A.V.

For Wossi

—D.J.

I think your buffalo is trying to tell you something.

He was born to play drums. You have to teach him how.

People may think that's silly. But you must be used to that.
Did anyone say, "Hey, that's a really great idea!" when you
brought a baby buffalo home?

But once they got to know your buffalo . . . that changed.

Everyone loves your buffalo! He's so sweet. And fun.

And fantastically shaggy!

He's probably really, really talented, too.

Has your buffalo always loved music?

Does he hum when he's
cleaning his room?

Sing in the shower?

Has he written a symphony?

(Joking! Most buffaloes don't write their first symphonies until middle school.)

How's his rhythm?

Did he dance to the beat at Baby Rocks! music class?

Does he clap along when he hears his favorite song?

No? Don't worry. Clapping is so tricky with hooves.

But that's okay.

Drumming *teaches* rhythm!

But wait. You're unsure.

You're thinking about his closet.

Look inside.

Four ice skates.

A surfboard.

That magic kit.

How-to-speak-Chinese CDs.

Scuba gear.

"It's different this time," your

buffalo whines in his buffalo way.

(Tell your buffalo not

to whine.)

Why not give it a try?!

说汉语
SPEAK
CHINESE

说汉语
SPEAK
CHINESE

说汉语
SPEAK
CHINESE

Are you worried about all the time he'll spend drumming?

The lessons?

The practicing?

And how once he gets good, and maybe joins a band,

he won't have time
to skateboard?

Go to the library?

Graze?

Stop worrying. This is going
to be great!

Set up your buffalo's drum set.

Does he have a good stool to sit on?

This can be a challenge.

Be creative.

(Your buffalo is so lucky! All those extra body parts
to help him balance!)

Ready?

Okay, hand him two drumsticks.

He may have trouble holding them at first.

Don't let your buffalo get frustrated!

Cheer him on! Encourage him!

Of course, you can also try yarn.

Now, let's get that buffalo drumming!

You might not know this, but drums can be kind of loud.

And when a buffalo's involved, well, that's loud times twelve!

You'll want to find a room that has been soundproofed.

If you can't, just give earplugs and earmuffs to everyone in your house.

And on your block.

Wow! Look at him go! He's a natural!

What big sound!

He has mighty power! Buffalo power!

That kind of talent is meant to be shared.

He should join the school band!

Your buffalo will get to perform with other
musicians as talented as he is.
He'll discover the magic of a band.

The way all those different sounds

combine to create one
amazing sound.

TOOT!

BANG!

TWEET!

S T

(If the magic's not happening, those earmuffs might come in handy.)

Some people think that being the loudest isn't the

most important part of being a good bandmate.

Your buffalo isn't one of those people.

He puts his heart and soul

and massive buffalo body

into every rehearsal.

They'll be ready for the big show in no time!

And what's more thrilling than a school band concert?

Shhhhh! They're getting ready to perform.

What a big moment!

Look at your buffalo! Look at the audience!

This is so exciting!

Get your camera!

Um.

I think your buffalo's trying to tell you something.